the five people you meet in HELL

the five people you meet in

HELL

An Unauthorized Parody

Rich Pablum

ATRIA BOOKS
New York London Toronto Sydney

ATRIA BOOKS
1230 Avenue of the Americas
New York, NY 10020

This book is a work of fiction. Names, characters, places and
incidents are products of the author's imagination or are used
fictitiously. Any resemblance to actual events or locales or
persons, living or dead, is entirely coincidental.

Copyright © 2005 by Billy Frolick

Library of Congress Cataloging-in-Publication Data
is available.

ISBN: 0-7432-7960-3

First Atria Books hardcover printing May 2005

10 9 8 7 6 5 4 3 2 1

ATRIA BOOKS is a trademark of Simon & Schuster, Inc.

Designed by Julie Schroeder

Manufactured in the United States of America

For information regarding special discounts for bulk purchases,
please contact Simon & Schuster Special Sales at 1-800-456-6798
or business@simonandschuster.com.

For Gabriel

a devil
of an angel

pier pressure

Have you ever noticed that sometimes the conclusion of a story comes at the beginning? Not just in pretentious movies from the seventies, either. In literature (that's "books," if you're under thirty), it's a manipulative ploy designed to pique the reader's interest in what is basically a shopworn detective story, dreary science fiction saga, or clichéd Western.

Or, in this case, a hackneyed morality tale. But, hey, one man's "hackneyed" is another's "profound." Who even knows what the word *hackneyed* means? Some movie critic probably dreamed it up, and now every amateur Roger Ebert drags it out just because he got sick of reading subtitles and fell asleep.

But I digress.

Edgy's final few hours on Earth took place at Angeli Pier, a midway that should have been condemned sometime during the Harding administration. The pier was located near Mykell Bay, a tourist trap that was expensive, shallow, and culturally insignificant.

Like most such eyesores, the pier was a magnet for social misfits. You know, the types you find pouring sugar directly into their mouths at Starbucks. Delusional transient philosophers who claim the end is near, and have the body odor to prove it.

It didn't take a DNA test to figure out that in addition to steroids and growth hormones, the carnival life was in Edgy's blood. He loved it all. The rickety rides. The unfair games and their deceitful operators. Children with the innocence of an Anne Geddes calendar shooting twelve-inch basketballs at eleven-inch hoops. Ah, yes. 'Twas ever thus. Not a thing had changed at Angeli Pier in decades, from the carnies' filthy clothes to the rancid oil the french fries were cooked in.

It was all wonderful to Edgy. After a shift at the pier, nothing thrilled him more than taking off his shoes at night, feeling something sticky on the bottom, and not knowing its origin. He experienced moments like this with the fervor of Bill O'Reilly in a private office with a free calling card.

The new attraction at the pier was a ride called Do Not Enter–Under Construction. It looked exactly like a ride that had occupied the same spot for years, the Krazy Kozmic Koaster. Edgy wondered why the powers-that-be at Angeli thought a name change would boost attendance. But his was not to reason why. He had lobbied for a position in management years ago, but one slip–filling out the application in pastel sidewalk chalk–had cost him the job. Listing Mickey

Rourke as a personal reference probably didn't help, either.

Edgy refused to be bitter, however. What did he know about decision making? Do Not Enter had proven to be wildly successful with the young and illiterate.

Edgy was a sprightly ninety-one. Though his skin had long ago taken on the texture of a petrified Domino's pizza, his eyes still burned with a crimson that even hourly applications of Visine couldn't fade.

His neck was sturdy and his arms were strong. He wore a stylish brown shirt and shorts. The resulting look was every bit his own—think UPS meets Abercrombie & Fitch. Perfect for back to school. Sorry, no X-Large. Free shipping on all orders over $100. Visa and MasterCard accepted. (No sales tax in Florida.)

"Stay away from that guy," a wary father hissed through his smile, warning his little girl as Edgy waved at them. Everyone at the pier knew him. They could smell him from twenty paces. Several patrons had applied for restraining orders.

Edgy just had one of those faces you thought you might recognize from the convenience store, or behind the counter at the D.M.V., or the post office bulletin board. These were unpleasant associations for most people, but the man himself was unaware of inspiring such negative feelings. To Edgy, people were just people, and if most of them felt like hurling hard plastic souvenirs his way or running in the opposite direction when they saw him, then so be it.

The last few letters had worn off his PARK UPKEEP shirt, right below his embroidered name, making it difficult to read. Consequently, many of his regular acquaintances had their own moniker for their least favorite pier employee. "Edgy Kreep," they would mutter after he'd belch with his mouth open, or stick out his foot in an effort to trip one of their kids. "That guy is one Edgy Kreep."

not dead yet

About an hour before he bought the farm, Edgy rode Do Not Enter. A sign at the front of the attraction said, YOU MUST BE THIS STUPID TO GO ON THIS RIDE. Fortunately, he couldn't read very well, and bounded into the front car with the unbridled enthusiasm of Winona Ryder at a Saks Fifth Avenue Labor Day sale.

Click-clack-click-clack. The car climbed up the track. *Click-clack-click-clack.* "Excuse me, Edgy Kreep," an eleven-year-old boy asked him.

"Could you please adjust your dentures so they stop making that annoying sound?"

"Hey, kid," Edgy said, scowling. "How'd you like me to make like Max Schmeling and pummel ya senseless?"

"First of all, dude, your archaic references are, like, totally lost on me. Second of all, my dad's a lawyer, so if I were you I'd seriously bag the physical threats."

"What kind of law?" Edgy asked. "Criminal? Litigation?"

"Worse," said the kid. "Entertainment."

Suddenly, the ride didn't seem scary at all.

Edgy knew how mean kids could get. As a boy, he'd had a sibling who called him names and beat him mercilessly. The fact that it was his younger sister made the years of suffering that much more humiliating. "You'll never amount to anything," Joanne would say.

But Edgy proved her wrong, becoming a part-time custodian at the decrepit seaside tourist trap. Joanne, meanwhile, had to settle for becoming a top-rated cardiac surgeon whose congressman husband remained faithful over forty-five years of marriage. She also had one of those black American Express cards, which she used with Impunity. Impunity was Joanne's prized toy poodle, who traveled everywhere with her.

After the coaster ride, Edgy went down to the janitors' break room, where his coworker, Flamingo, had an open can of grease, a magazine called *Farm Fun,* and a guilty look on his face.

"Nothing," Flamingo said.

"What?" asked Edgy.

"I'm not doing anything," said the trembling young man. "I swear."

"Relax, Flamingo," Edgy said. "I'm just getting a cup of coffee. Then you can go back to whatever you were doing—"

"Which was nothing."

Edgy shook his head as he limped over to the coffee machine. "You ought to consider getting your medication adjusted, amigo."

Flamingo sat down and joined Edgy. "By the way, Happy Arbor Day," he said. "What are you doing to celebrate?"

Edgy's family had always made a big deal about Arbor Day, and his memories were not especially pleasant. "I'm gonna see how much Wild Turkey I can throw back without passing out."

"Sounds like a plan."

Edgy headed out again to wander aimlessly around the pier. Once upon a time, Angeli Pier had been a real hot spot, teeming with libidinous energy and beautiful women. But the business had changed. Now the only big busts he saw involved drugs, and the only erection he was familiar with was that of the strip mall going up across the street.

In the old days, a canvas tent at the pier had featured world-renowned Siamese twins; now there were two Jewish cousins who operated the gift shop. Across the strand, the World's Smallest Midget (who died of shortness of breath) had been replaced by a four-year-old boy with a bad cough. Where the bearded lady once sat, sadly, now dozed a man with a mangy goatee. The last newsworthy event took place when some guy ate a cheesesteak sandwich that had been out in the sun too long.

This was all about to change. As unsuspecting patrons were shuttled through the Do Not Enter entrance, Edgy sat in his usual shaded corner of the midway. It was behind the Tommy Lee, a long train of hardened steel, which was called the Roddy McDowall in the 1980s, the Forrest Tucker in the 1970s, and the Uncle Miltie in the 1960s. In the 1950s, it was where musicians went to shoot smack, avoid their wives, and occasionally smack or shoot their wives.

Ironically, it's where Edgy had first met Marginelle.

love's in fashion

The year was 1952. For Edgy, much of it was still a blur. A gingham dress. Braided hair. Spike heels. It was a look Edgy was still experimenting with, but Marginelle—fortunately for him—had about as much talent judging men as Ben Affleck had picking film projects. (Granted, Ben wasn't around in those days, but come on—you can imagine the crap he would have done.)

Edgy and Marginelle eyed each other from across the midway.

"How'd ya like to cut a rug, honey?" he asked her, approaching eagerly.

She tilted her head and squinted. "I'd leave the back long and trim the sides," Marginelle replied in her thick Eastern European accent. "And for God's sake, lose the braids. Who are you, Willie Nelson?"

"First of all, this story takes place years before most people know who Willie Nelson is, let alone pot and income tax problems. And 'cutting a rug' is an expression," Edgy explained, rolling his eyes as the band started a new tune. "Anyone who talks as funny as you do must be familiar with the polka."

"I know a flush beats a straight," said Marginelle. "But the last time I played, all I had was a little pair."

"I hate to break it to you, honey, but you still do. Don't worry, though. *My* hands are plenty big."

Edgy thought he had been in love before, but the stinging he was feeling in his nether regions felt unusual. This time, it was like he was getting the STD first.

"Marginelle," Edgy said. "I'm feelin' a little queasy. I'm either smitten, or it's the four hot dogs on a stick I had for breakfast."

Marginelle, who was studying to be a nurse, thought fast. "Let's head over to that secluded area that smells like dead mussels."

She took his hand and led him to an observation point high above a section of the water frequented by killer sharks. "You know, I could let you seduce me all night," Marginelle said. "But if you feel like jumping, that would work, too."

"You read my mind, sister," Edgy moaned. "And if I don't find a Bromo-Seltzer pretty soon, it's gonna look like a pretty sweet option."

"Well, if you do decide to dive in, Tex, take the dress off first. I think it would fit my sister."

Instead, they headed over to an arcade game that combined fortune-telling with rating sexual prowess. Edgy dropped a nickel in the slot, gripped the handle, and squeezed as hard as he could.

"Mmm—'Flaccid,'" Marginelle read with obvious disappointment. The neon readout continued to climb higher. "Oh, here we go—'Proficiently potent' . . . 'A regular Don Juan' . . ."

"Keep reading," Edgy said, squeezing so hard that he had to close his eyes.

"'Predator' . . . 'Possible felon' . . . 'The next Mike Tyson' . . . 'Miss Hawaiian Tropic Judge' . . . ooohhhh, you made it all the way to the top. I can't even read you this one. It's too embarrassing."

"Just say it," Edgy grunted.

"'Future governor of California.'"

the fly in the ointment

That night, Edgy came home and woke up his younger sister, Joanne.

"How much do you need?" she asked groggily.

"Jo, this is important," Edgy said breathlessly. "I think I've met the love of my life."

"Everyone touches themselves," she said, rolling over. "It's nothing to feel guilty about."

Twenty minutes left prior to Edgy's feeding the worms. It's at this point that his tale is touched by another.

The story is one you might not think twice about if someone told it to you. In fact, there's a good chance you'd doze off faster than a Jew at a NASCAR event.

It involves a boy nicknamed Sticky. He had come to Angeli Pier on a gloomy August night a few weeks earlier. He'd ridden every ride with his friends: Splitting Headache, Psycho-Cyclone, Loose Bladder's Nightmare. But it was on the Krazy Kozmic Koaster that Sticky had made a fatal mistake.

His friends had all agreed to drop their pants when the flash camera went off at the end of the ride, a vertical plunge into water. But Sticky—who had a tendency to take things literally—removed his trousers and actually dropped them.

Down into the antiquated mechanism of the Krazy Kozmic Koaster—the bowels of the mother ship, as it were—went Sticky's faded Levi's 501s. Embarrassment followed. An arrest was made of the pants-free boy. The photo subsequently used in the security booth to identify Sticky, should he ever return, was of the naked buttocks of a confused teenager.

The Krazy Kozmic Koaster had been shut down for several days, after which it was renamed Do Not Enter.

Edgy watched now, as customers filed into the waiting area for the ride. As he did, a five-year-old boy approached him.

"Edgy Kreep?" the boy asked. "Is it true that you learned origami, the Japanese art of paper folding, during the war?"

"Yeah, it's true," Edgy grunted.

"Could you make me a dragon with a big tail?"

"You mean instead of an annoying little runt with a drippy nose?"

"Mommy," whined the kid. "This geriatric is using irony and sarcasm as an inappropriate outlet for his feelings of low self-esteem and disappointment in life. But I'm only five. I don't understand!"

Edgy pulled a small, square piece of paper out

of his pocket. The boy watched, fascinated, as Edgy folded it into a long, thin, nondescript shape.

"It's a drumstick," Edgy said, handing his creation to the boy. "Now, beat it!"

"You're a mean man," the boy said.

"Wait 'til you're my age, kid. I got hemorrhoids bigger than you."

Final words are a funny thing. Did Carl Jung really say, "Oh, to be Jung again"? And what about George Gipp's famous, "Win one for the Gipper"? And Tupac Shakur—could his dying words on the Las Vegas Strip really have been "Don't be touchin' da bling, yo"?

Edgy Kreep's last uttered sentence? What a doozy. No, seriously. That's what he said—"What a doozy!"

This followed a series of interesting noises. Do Not Enter, filled with passengers, starting its creaky climb. The waves crashing against the rocks below. The plates crashing in the employee lounge. Edgy's clicking dentures down below. The gusty wind blowing through Angeli Pier. The breaking wind coursing through the intestinal tracts of the snack-bar faithful. The thud of Do Not Enter's gears trying to grind through the zipper of Sticky's pants.

And then there were Edgy's last words, as he looked up to see the rear end of a grossly overweight woman directly above his head and on its way down.

"What a doozy!"

the end is rear

Edgy tried to radio Flamingo, but he knew this was an exercise in futility, as the original cast recording of *Rent* was undoubtedly blasting in the employee lounge. He thought about calling the police. He thought about reciting a Buddhist incantation to reverse the falling woman's direction.

Unfortunately, he thought of everything except moving out of the way.

Edgy remembered hearing horror stories about tragedies in other amusement parks. At Coney

Island, a young girl got her braces caught on the Tilt-A-Whirl. At Seven Flags Over Cleveland, a boy fell from the top of the Ferris wheel. And in one of the worst financial disasters in the history of the Walt Disney Company, a Disneyland patron once used a coupon for a discount admission.

Flamingo arrived and climbed the side of Do Not Enter, doing a lame imitation of Gene Kelly on the way up and taking several bows once he had reached the top. Edgy sighed; the kid wasn't going to be of any use.

You may wonder how all of this could have happened during the time it took a three-hundred-pound woman's body to plummet fifty feet. Well, the answer is that this is a book, my friend. So un-furrow your brow, wipe that disapproving smirk off your face, and suspend your disbelief a little. Okay? Terrific.

"Is that a human body?" Edgy asked, as the überposterior made its way toward his skull. "Or has Jupiter dropped from the sky?"

The assembled crowd laughed. Perhaps this

was some novel form of street entertainment, they collectively thought. (After all, this was a crummy seaside arcade, not Harvard.)

"Crack all the jokes you want," the falling woman called to Edgy. "Just don't move an inch, unless you want to supervise the biggest cleanup since the day after the Red Sox victory parade."

For someone who was ostensibly plunging to her death, the obese woman's comic timing was impeccable. In fact, a local arts critic in the crowd made a note that with Totie Fields gone, Roseanne pretty much retired, and Margaret Cho all skinny again, there was definitely room in the stand-up world for a new weight-challenged comedienne. If she lived—let alone be able to "stand up"—he thought, maybe this is the one.

Time was running out for Edgy. He saw a white light. Then a black light. He saw multi-colored socks, for some reason. Edgy realized that he was looking at a Benetton billboard. When he turned his gaze back directly overhead, all he could see was the gigantic end that would be his . . . well, end. Talk about a keister, he thought. This ass could apply for statehood.

"What a doozy!" he said.

And those, just to recap, were the last words Edgy spoke.

today is arbor day

We are in 1908, in the delivery room of a medical clinic that should have been torn down years earlier. This place is so filthy that the nurses chain-smoke.

Edgy's mother lights up a cigarette herself as she watches her newborn acclimate to the world. "What a shame," she tells her husband.

"They all look like that," Edgy's father replies. "Somewhere between Winston Churchill, Alfred Hitchcock, and Fred Mertz."

"I have no idea what any of that just meant," Edgy's mother responds. "What I was talking about is how unfortunate it is that Edgy had to be born on Arbor Day. It's every kid's nightmare. You want your birthday to be special, and all the world can think about is the inspiration *of Julius Sterling Morton, the Nebraska journalist who devoted his life to bettering agricultural techniques and awareness. He even served under Grover Cleveland as his secretary of agriculture. But Morton's greatest legacy is undoubtedly Arbor Day, the first of which took place on April 10, 1872, and—*

"Wake up, Harold! I'm talking to you!"

somewhere
in a handbasket

There is much conjecture about how one makes the trek from the here-and-now to, as we say, "other worlds." Is there a long tunnel with an aura of white light at the end? Are you welcomed by docile, winged figures and escorted to a wondrous new place? Or is it more of a motorized walkway leading to a crowded baggage carousel, like at the Reno airport?

For Edgy, there was a clear sense, immediately, that his overdue library books were no longer going to be an issue. Either he had perished, or that smell was the sardine sandwich he had stuffed in his pocket and forgotten a few days earlier.

Immediately after the accident, Edgy felt a weight lifted from him, literally and figuratively. At first all he could see was various shades of red and glittering silver. Perhaps he was on the set of a Baz Luhrmann movie. But, alas, no one broke into a pop song medley. The sky was stripes of mauve, chartreuse, and eggshell, with charcoal highlights. He sensed a distinct possibility that he had wound up in the Ralph Lauren paint catalogue. The clouds moved in bizarre patterns, ultimately forming the words, "I've got good news and bad news."

Edgy's newfound weightlessness brought on considerable motion sickness and triggered his old acid reflux problem. But the idea of flying without waiting in line for two hours, removing his shoes, and having to show his ID to seven different people *was* appealing,

What happened? he wondered. He thought about the fat woman falling toward him, his arthritic hands shooting up in desperation, the crowd rooting for a violent, gory finish.

Did she just bounce off of me and live?

Am I the reason she didn't die?

Did I leave the oven on when I left the house?

Is there life after death?

Did Jason Alexander really *need to do KFC commercials after nine seasons on* Seinfeld*?*

What bothered Edgy most was that every physical and emotional malady he had ever suffered during his time on Earth seemed to have returned in spades. The migraine headache. The sciatica. The cramp in his left calf. The itching. The swelling.

He thought getting old was bad. Death, at this point, was just plain sucky.

thursday with harry

It is 1927. Edgy is a teenager. Uncle Harry's apartment is messy, and there is leftover food everywhere and a sink full of dishes. Such is the life of an unmarried yo-yo salesman.

Harry and his uncle are listening to the World Series on a cathedral radio. The Yankees are looking like a good bet to win.

"I hear they're paying that Gehrig kid thirty-five dollars a year," says Uncle Harry, shaking his head as he closes the newspaper. "I just hate that they're buying the team."

Uncle Harry moves closer to Edgy. "What a beautiful day!" he exclaims. "Know what I'd like to do?"

"Sleep with Ruby Keeler?" Edgy asks innocently.

"Who told you that?" demands Harry.

"You said it last week after you'd had your fourth navy grog."

Harry walked over to a cabinet in the corner. "Look, kid. Booze has great health benefits. For one thing, I've never slept better than after throwing back a bottle of whiskey. For another, I have a feeling that hooch thins the blood. And secondly, look at French people—they eat all that rich food, and they're the healthiest people on earth."

"Americans really love the French people," says Edgy.

"And they always will, kid," predicts Uncle Harry, straining a martini. "Now, how about giving me one of those swell massages?"

if you lived in highwater, you'd be home by now

When Edgy came to, he found he had become the target in a shooting gallery much like the one on Angeli Pier. He was surrounded by plastic ducks. His back was killing him. And a lineup of brats was shooting BBs at his face.

Edgy had a growing suspicion that he was not in heaven. He had yet to see a gate, pearly or otherwise. There was a distinct lack of angels (though there was a hooker named Angel he thought he recognized). No choirs were singing.

Still, he was willing to entertain the notion that his current dwelling was merely a transitional area. Maybe heaven was, as they say, "backed up." There certainly seemed to be endless requests made by people for entry, not to mention for their pets. Perhaps there was some kind of online registration he could pursue to expedite things. He'd Google "Heaven" and go from there. Obviously, there was some kind of administrative glitch.

Yeah, right.

The weird part was that Angeli Pier had deteriorated even further. It was barely inhabited, dark, musty, and smelled like a full clothes hamper.

Some signage he had never noticed before seemed to indicate other changes as well. HELL'S BACKYARD, read one. HELL–2 MILES, said another. H-E-DOUBLE HOCKEY STICKS IS REAL CLOSE, the third promised.

None of this dispelled Edgy's faith that he was headed for a peaceful and placid world, a place free of lower back pain.

Crawling his way out of the shooting gallery, Edgy noticed that the kids had disappeared and the midway was empty. Then he heard a voice calling in the distance.

"Mr. Kreep?"

He turned to see a fortyish woman in a yellow sport coat heading his way on high heels.

"Yeah?"

"C. Alice LeVitra," she said, extending a well-manicured hand that, fortunately, happened to be her own. "Welcome to Highwater. I'm heading up the Chamber of Commerce."

"Hold on—did you say 'Highwater'?" Edgy repeated. "As in 'Come hell or . . .'?"

"Oh, we tend to downplay that whole thing," C. Alice said. "Why focus on the negative? Highwater has really developed its own identity, and we're not playing second fiddle to—uh, that *other* place—anymore. Our schools are top-rated, we have a new ballfield . . . we've even got our own water supply. And the homes are so affordable! May I show you a few?"

"Oh, now I get it—the yellow jacket . . . the whiny voice . . . the pushy attitude. You sell real estate . . ."

"Well, actually, yellow jackets are just the style here. As for the real estate thing, that's more of a side interest. As I said, I'm very active with the Chamber. I'm all about working to make the community stronger than ever.

"But now that I think about it, there *is* a fabulous little two-bedroom with a fireplace about two blocks away. Just came on the market today. It's a fixer-upper or a teardown—it's up to you, and I can recommend a contractor who is not only good, but *fast*. We could walk over, or I could drive you . . . hey, where're you going?"

Edgy hit the highway. As he walked, he noticed a series of billboards reading YOU'RE GETTING HOTTER . . . GO TO HELL! On the back of each was a photo of C. Alice and the line, YOU'RE GETTING COLDER . . . TASTE HIGHWATER LIFE!

Edgy had seen more than one novelty book that made a point that there was an actual town in

the United States named Hell. Certain that the billboards were promoting the town, he trudged on.

A bright red Kia slowed to a stop near Edgy.
The driver, a middle-aged white man, leaned his
head out.

"Whazzup?" he said.

Edgy rolled his eyes.

"Homeboy, I be talkin' to yo' ass," the voice
continued.

Oh, brother, Edgy thought, this is even worse.
It's not enough that this guy is driving a Kia, he's
also using outdated urban patois as a way to seem
hip.

Edgy began to trot. But the sad truth was that, in
his condition, he couldn't outrun a snail, or even a
Kia. The car—and its annoying driver—drew closer.

"Dude, what's the four-one-one?"

"Look," Edgy said. "I need a little alone time,
okay?"

"I'm down with that, bro," the man said.

"Who are you?" Edgy asked, his curiosity getting the best of him.

"Maurice Towne, y'all. But you can call my bad self 'Mo.'"

"Mo Towne?" Edgy groaned. "God, no."

Mo opened the passenger door and Edgy got in.

By now, Edgy thought he had put it all together. But he needed confirmation.

"So what's the deal with you?"

"You mean 'What the dilly-o'? It's simple. I'm the first person you encounter here. I'm *The White Guy Who Insists on Peppering His Speech with Hip-Hop Lingo.*"

Edgy gritted his teeth, took a deep breath, then introduced himself.

"I'm Edgy."

"Ya got dat right."

"Do you think you could help me with some directions?" Edgy asked. "I need to, um . . . *get as far away from you as possible.*"

"Damn, dat be *cold*," said Mo.

"I'm not joking," Edgy insisted. "You're seriously giving me the willies, here. If I wasn't grappling with major theological issues right now and obsessed with whether I was living or dead and had gone to heaven or hell, I'd knock your block off."

The car entered the town of Hell, which Edgy again recognized as the Angeli Pier's midway.

"*Oy gevalt,*" he said, getting out of the car.

A SPECIAL MESSAGE FROM
AUTHOR RICH PABLUM

⋇

First of all, I'm sorry that this note couldn't be personalized. I've found that the more I can make individual contact with my readers, the better the—what's the word . . . oh, yeah—sales.

That's why I'm embarking on a national tour this summer to promote The Five People You Meet in Hell. *No need to commit to attending in your area quite yet, but keep in mind that it should be quite a scene. We're thinking of having sushi platters. Do you like sushi? I hated it until I started getting published and going to New York a lot. The town is sushi-crazed, let me tell you. I'm not a big fan of halibut, and salmon can get kind of stringy. But fatty tuna? Yum.*

Anyway, I probably shouldn't even be thinking about

the tour when the book isn't even half finished. I mean, Edgy just got to you-know-where, for crying out loud.

I hope you're enjoying The Five People You Meet in Hell *as much as I sincerely think you should if you believe in love and the human spirit.*

If you don't believe in those things, you deserve whatever horrible crap befalls you. Not that I'm playing whatssisname or anything. I got enough trouble trying to figure out where to find edible sushi in Lincoln, Nebraska.

is it hot in here,
or is it hell?

Edgy strolled down the midway, which was still bizarrely deserted. Several large billboards bore the face of actor George Kennedy, and the line, LET'S WIPE OUT LACTOSE INTOLERANCE IN OUR LIFETIME.

At the north end of the midway, Edgy was surprised to see that a superstore had been erected. He didn't remember one being constructed, let alone one that was a full city block in size. A huge sign read, BRIMSTONE WAL-MART—YOU'D SWEAR YOU WERE BACK ON EARTH.

Edgy was glad he wasn't driving. Cars were backed up for blocks, and validations were given only for people who could name *anyone* from the current cast of *Saturday Night Live*.

"The fat guy . . ." he heard a woman in a two-door Kia say, with obvious uncertainty.

"Which fat guy?" the booth attendant asked suspiciously.

"I don't know!" the woman barked, as the line of Kias behind her honked their horns.

"Well, there's *always* a fat guy. That's like saying, 'The homely, talentless chick.' Or 'The black guy who doesn't get any decent material.' Sixteen-fifty, please."

"Jeez—I can get a pair of socks at Banana Republic for that."

Much as Edgy found this exchange riveting, he was curious to venture into the Brimstone Wal-Mart and explore its offerings. He stood before a large map that informed him, "You are here—tough luck!"

A craving for caffeine suddenly overcame Edgy. He made his way off the broken escalator to a section called Java the Hutt. Edgy considered boycotting it because of its cutesy name, but the smell of overroasted beans called out to him.

Edgy had never seen anything like the scene inside. The coffeehouse was packed with people between fifteen and twenty-three, wearing unattractive, open-toed footwear and toe rings, and either talking loudly on cell phones or pretending to work on laptop computers as they eyed one another. They sat on wooden chairs that resembled—but were less comfortable than—those used in a police interrogation room.

Around the paneled café snaked a line of customers who waited as the twenty-year-old barista—listening to an iPod—recounted the previous night's episode of *American Idol* to his roommate. On the counter was a tip jar stuffed like a tomboy on prom night.

"How are you?" Edgy asked the girl behind the register after a half-hour wait. The clerk had little flowers painted on her fingernails.

"Super," she said.

"Any recommendations?" Edgy asked.

"Well, we have a mocha latte that's really

super, and omigod, the coconut-mint blended is superdelicious."

Edgy looked at the girl's name tag. "The Second Person You Meet," it read: *"The Store Employee Who Constantly Says 'Super!'"*

"Okay, I'll take the coconut thing," Edgy said.

"Super, then . . . is that for here or to go?"

"To go, please."

"Super. Six seventy-five."

"Six seventy-five?" Edgy repeated incredulously. "What is this—the airport?"

He handed her a bill.

"Out of ten? Super," the girl said, giving Edgy his change. "You have a super day, now."

Go suck an egg, Edgy thought, as he ventured across the floor of the mall. There was nothing he hated more than relentlessly positive young people who had no idea what life had in store for them.

"sin"-ema

Edgy knew that he needed to engage in a mind-less activity to help calm his nerves. As luck would have it, Brimstone Wal-Mart did have a movie theater.

"What's playing?" Edgy asked the theater manager (also known as *the third person he meets*).

"Oh, you came on a good day," he replied. "We're running a festival."

"Of . . ."

"The Films of Chris Columbus."

"Who?"

"Chris Columbus. The most successful director of his generation. Come on in—*Heartbreak Hotel* starts in about ten minutes."

"Hang on—this Chris Columbus guy worked with Elvis?"

"No, no," the manager explained. "But his identification with the Presley legacy compelled him to write and direct this film. It's the story of a precocious teenager who kidnaps the King and brings him back to his house so that his mom—played by Tuesday Weld—can successfully be brought to orgasm."

"And Elvis is played by . . .?"

"The guy who hangs himself in *An Officer and a Gentleman.*"

"That sounds absolutely vile," Edgy said. "Is it a drama?"

"As it turns out, yes."

"What else are you showing?"

"Well, there's *Mrs. Doubtfire*. See, Sally Field and Robin Williams are married, and—"

"Stop."

"Hmmm," the manager sighed, perusing his

schedule. "I guess we can rule out *Bicentennial Man,* then . . ." He scratched his head. "How about *Only the Lonely*?"

"Do I even want to hear a description of that one?"

"It's basically a straight retread of *Marty,* minus a script, believable performances, and filmmaking talent. I will give Columbus credit for one thing, though. He found a more unappealing romantic lead than the star of the original, Ernest Borgnine–John Candy."

"This was before Candy died, I assume?"

"Based on the performance, I really couldn't tell you."

"And Candy seduces what?" asked the fascinated Edgy. "A sixty-pound side of beef?"

"You're closer than you think. Candy's love interest is none other than waifish Brat Packer Ally Sheedy. Whatcha think? Want to give it a shot?"

"I'm gonna pass," Edgy said. "I'd rather have a ménage à trois with Linda Tripp and Greta Van Susteren."

"Well, do try to stop by next week," the manager suggested. "We're running Woody Allen's films from the past decade, and there are prizes for anyone who stays awake for longer than fifteen minutes. Then it's *Analyze That,* something called *Saving Silverman,* a movie with David Arquette and a dog, and the two *Matrix* sequels."

But Edgy was gone. After meandering around Wal-Mart for several more hours, he made his way to the Information Desk.

"Excuse me," he asked *the fourth person he meets,* an older woman at the station. "Can you tell me where I am?"

"Where do you think you are?" she asked.

"Don't tell me you answer every question with a question," Edgy pleaded.

"Why would you say that?" the woman asked.

"I just—everyone I've run into so far has been annoying in one way or the other . . . using urban phrases, repeating the word *super* over and over, describing Chris Columbus movies. Would it be overly paranoid of me to call it a 'conspiracy of evil'?"

"*Now* who's asking the questions?" the woman countered.

"It's my right to ask questions!" the overly caffeinated Edgy insisted. "And you are an Information Desk employee!"

"Who's next?" asked the woman, looking through the man before her as though he didn't even exist.

dying for a drink

Edgy worked his way down to the ground floor of the Brimstone Wal-Mart, where a Denny's was flanked–for some reason–by two identical Olive Garden restaurants. It was a toss-up: inedible food versus unlimited bread.

Instead, he wandered into a sports bar called Thirst and Ten, which trumpeted something called a "Butt-Kickin' Happy Hour."

Inside were a dozen twentysomethings, mostly male, drinking overpriced American draft beer and wearing T-shirts featuring "humorous" slogans.

TOO DRUNK TO SCREW, read one. GRADUATE, BUD-
WEISER U, said another. On each of the seventeen
monitors was an exhibition baseball game between
the Cleveland Indians and the Philadelphia Phillies
that had gone into extra innings.

As he took a stool, Edgy noticed that the bartender was . . . well, red. Not red like an Indian
from a fifties TV show or a communist, but bright,
fire engine red.

This would have been remarkable enough if
the guy were *not* Dick Cheney's doppelgänger.

Edgy breathed a sigh of relief. Obviously, if
Dick Cheney were here, this couldn't be hell. This
was just a peculiar situation that would soon explain
itself. Edgy had merely wandered into an area of
town with which he was unfamiliar. His parched
condition had driven him to a sports-viewing em-
porium where the bartender was a red-dyed Dick
Cheney lookalike. Simple explanation.

"What'll it be, pal?" he asked.

"Moonlighting?" Edgy hinted, wary of seeming
too open about his suspicion that this guy—The *fifth
person*—was the vice president of the United States.

"Ah, yes," said the bartender. "Moonlighting—two shots of peach schnapps, a finger of Wild Turkey, and sweet cream over ice. One Moonlighting coming right up."

Edgy felt his signature queasiness moving in again as he watched the barkeep concoct the vile libation. But Edgy was on a mission, and he would not let unsavory beverage combinations impede his progress.

"Mmmm," he cooed, bringing the drink to his lips. "So—wonder what the weather in *Wyoming* is like right now?"

The bartender stopped wiping the counter and stared Edgy down.

"You must be looking for the Non Sequiturs Anonymous meeting," he said. "Either that, or you think I'm actually interested in talking to you."

"Just trying to be friendly," Edgy demurred, not even completely certain what "demurring" was.

"You want to be friendly? Express yourself with green paper," the bartender suggested, pointing to a jar that said, "Tipping Isn't a City in China."

Edgy couldn't take the suspense anymore.

"You wouldn't by any chance be nicknamed 'Second in Command,' would you?" Edgy asked El Hombre Rojo.

"Only in the bedroom," the bartender said, lowering his voice. "Tell you what—meet me in the park across the street tomorrow afternoon and I'll tell you everything. If there's anything to tell, that is."

"Oooh—you're not merely a red-skinned Dick Cheney lookalike who works as a suds monkey in a crappy sports bar, you're also cryptic. Ya got me on the edge of my seat, here, Tonto."

"Okay, pal," the bartender said. "I'm cuttin' you off."

Tired and with limited funds, Edgy made his way to a street called Motel Row. It turned out to be aptly named, for though there were a half-dozen such establishments, every one of them was a Comfort Inn.

"Welcome to Comfort Inn number seven," said the desk clerk, who was playing solitaire on his iBook. "How can I help you today?"

"Hmm. Well, maybe you can do the math. I've got about sixty bucks and a burning desire to sleep in a cracker box that reeks of carpet disinfectant."

"Sir, I believe you're in the right place."

The clerk gave Edgy a list of local restaurants, two room keys, and a painter's mask. "Can I tell you about our Continental breakfast?"

"Sure—as long as I don't have to eat it," Edgy replied.

"Very good, sir," the clerk said with a chuckle. "But I think you might be pleasantly surprised. To start things off, we feature weak coffee, lukewarm hot chocolate, and a selection of Lipton teas. From there, we offer a choice between overripe oranges, underripe bananas, and canned peaches. Eating the croissants will require the incisors of a barracuda, as will consuming either of our wide 'selection' of stale breakfast cereal, which consists of Rice Krispies and corn flakes. Also, you'll probably be shoehorned between two families of tourists composed of flu-ridden kids, controlling mothers, and fathers who talk about nothing but Tiger Woods. Don't be surprised if we start vacuuming or remodeling during your meal. And if you smell something a little off, well, I'm sure you've already, uh, *gotten wind* that everyone around here is lactose intolerant . . ?"

"Thanks a bunch," Edgy said, heading for the elevator. "I have a feeling I'm going to be pretty desperate tomorrow morning, so the breakfast ought to work out well."

Edgy's room fully met his expectations. A colony of flies greeted him as he entered. A construction crew jackhammered against the wall from the adjacent room (at least he *hoped* it was a construction crew).

He had expected to crash out, but wondering whether he was dead or not—and if so, which realm of the afterworld he had landed in—had taken a psychological toll. After looking through the dresser drawers with the fervent hope that the previous guest had left behind prescription drugs, Edgy flicked on the television.

A logo identified the first station he found as the Alan Thicke Channel. The *Growing Pains* evening block had just ended; now airing was a Rose Bowl parade Thicke had cohosted with Karen Valentine in the mid-nineties.

On Deathtime, identified as "The First Network for Deceased Women," Lindsay Wagner was starring in a movie about a former actress who had become addicted to appearing in automobile commercials. Following that was the premiere of *Trading Faces*, a makeover show in which women who couldn't afford Botox received DNA replacement from those who had abused it. The hosts were Melanie Griffith and Meg Ryan.

Edgy switched over to the Gaming Network. *Larry King's Strip Poker Extravaganza* was in full swing; tonight the talk-show host was pitted against Linda Hunt, Edward Asner, Carmen Electra, Larry Flynt, Estelle Getty, and Mimi Rogers.

Poker? He remembered his first conversation with Marginelle about that fickle game. Was there a reason it was now staring him in the face? And, hey–that Linda Hunt doesn't have a bad figure . . .

Waking up in hell was beginning to seem like an acceptable fate.

for a dead guy,
you don't look half bad

Edgy headed to the local park the following afternoon. He waited for three and a half hours before the red-skinned bartender showed up.

"Well, if it isn't the *late* Dick Cheney."

"Good one," the guy said, sitting down next to Edgy on the bench. "And here I thought all of the hacks were writing for Jimmy Kimmel and Jay Leno."

"Okay, out with it," Edgy said. "Are you Dick Cheney or not?"

"Yeah, I'm Cheney," said the crimson man.

"Then this isn't hell . . ." Edgy surmised.

"*That* I can't tell you."

"But—but—but . . ."

The red man slapped Edgy across the face. "Listen—you wanted the truth, but it's not pretty. Now, you think you can handle it?"

Edgy took a deep breath. "Go."

"Do you remember all of the health problems I was having during Dubya's first term?" he began. "There were several heart-related episodes? And I was taken to—"

"—an 'undisclosed location'!" Edgy chimed in.

"Right," said the Man Who Would Be Cheney. "That was code for the afterlife. For obvious reasons, though, we weren't going to leak that piece of information."

Edgy got up and started pacing. "This is unbelievable," he said. "What you're saying is, you died, and—"

"Let me backtrack a little. There was a point at which we knew I was going to go. The Joint Chiefs were all out of 'joint'—heh-heh—because once I croaked, Dubya would actually have to make tougher decisions than which book to read to a bunch of schoolkids.

"Karl Rove developed a plan, which began with a secret, midnight screening of *Weekend at Bernie's*."

"*Weekend at Bernie's?*" asked a stunned Edgy. "The movie?"

"No, genius—the opera."

"With Andrew McCarthy?"

"Right. And don't forget Jonathan Silverman," Cheney added. "Jonny did some of his finest work in *Bernie's*."

"Okay," Edgy said, trying to keep his breathing strong and steady. "Let's get back to how you ended up here."

"Right," agreed Cheney. "Are you familiar with the film's story line?"

"It's not exactly Steinbeck," said Edgy. "McCarthy and Silverman are staying at an uncle's house on the beach. The guy drops dead, and—*no way!*"

"Way."

"You're telling me that you died, and the Bush administration perpetuated the illusion that you were alive?"

"As they do to this day. Look at some of the footage of me at press conferences, or just strolling the White House lawn with Lynn."

He shook his head. "The poor thing. She's getting bursitis from holding that stick in my ass."

Edgy was dumbfounded. Here was the true meaning of the term *puppet regime*. While John Kerry was being accused of wooing Hollywood during the '04 presidential race, little did the voting public know that Bush and Co. were receiving covert inspiration from Hollywood B movies of the mid-eighties. It wasn't difficult to believe, but it was going to take some time to truly comprehend.

"And your skin?" Edgy asked.

"Oh, the full-body dye is just a bad pun," Cheney admitted. "You see, now I know I'll always be in a 'red state.'"

"I never knew you were such a cutup," Edgy said. "You kill me."

"So to speak." Cheney winked.

"Right."

saturday with lori

It is 1997. Edgy is eighty-nine years old.

He is sitting on the small balcony of his apartment, listening to the Bible on tape (read by Steve Buscemi) and whittling a shark's tooth into a shark's nose.

A Kia drives up, clearly in need of a new transmission. The car sputters, then coasts to the curb.

The driver's-side door opens, and a girl in her thirties comes out. She is wearing a halter top and stiletto heels. Looking around, she sees that the street is deserted. Hearing one of her favorite biblical passages, she looks up to the balcony and sees the old man.

"Hello," she says. "I'm Lori Smelling."

"What do you want?"

"You could start with your name."

"Edgy Kreep, that's me."

"You ain't kidding."

"We don't like your type around here," Edgy snarls, setting down his whittling.

"And what type would that be?"

"Professionals."

Lori is taken aback. It's not the first time she's been mistaken for a cheap hooker.

"I'm no flesh peddler!" she explains. "Have you ever heard of a little TV show called Brentwood 90402*?"*

"Don't have a television," Edgy says. "I don't go in for that kind of thing."

"Well, I do happen to be a 'professional'—a professional actor*—and an heirer to boot. I could buy and sell you, grandpa, and this whole backwoods town of yours."*

"Hang on a second, there, missy—what's this 'actor' and 'heirer' business?"

*"*Actress *is an outdated term. There need not be any gender distinction made for a performer. I'm now lobbying that the word* heiress *be abolished as well, in favor of the nonsexist* heirer*. Also, my father is paying off the* E! Channel *and* Premiere *magazine, which should help."*

"*Heirer, eh? Rolls right off the tongue,*" Edgy says. "*Well, in* that *outfit, don't be surprised if someone calls you 'heifer' instead.*" *He chuckles as Lori tucks herself back into her halter. "From the looks of it, you're* definitely *in SAG.*"

"*That's a real knee-slapper, grandpa. You look like you've been around the block once or twice yourself,*" says Lori. "*Any chance you can give me a tour of this godforsaken burg, or is the whittling just too enthralling?*"

"*I guarantee it beats watching you tear up the floorboards,*" Edgy says, grabbing his coat. "*And by the way, if you hate it here so much, why the interest?*"

"*Research. I'm up for the lead in an Oxygen original M.O.W.,* Mary Jo Buttofuoco: The Early Years. "

i'll show you
how to connect, bub

"Everything in the world is connected," began a tiny but very serious man Edgy met on his way out of the park. "My responsibility is to explain this to you."

"Yeah, yeah, I know," Edgy said, pushing him out of the way. "The whole Kevin Bacon thing."

"Never heard that one," the man said as he slowly got back on his feet. "I'm talking about the tides and the moon, man . . . longitude and latitude . . . fat-free potato chips and anal leakage."

"I see," said Edgy. "Seems that you're a true master of the obvious."

"I should hope so. Majored in it in college. Now, you wanna talk about a great movie?" he continued. "My pick would be *Citizen Kane.*"

"Uh-huh . . ."

"And when it comes to seafood, I think lobster can't be beat."

"Evil world leaders?"

"Hitler was absolutely awful," said the man.

"Cola?"

"I consider Coke Classic to be at the top of the heap. Sells very well, too, from what I understand."

"Musical groups?"

"I'm a huge Beatles fan."

"Salad?"

"Hail, Caesar!"

"You are a learned man," Edgy deadpanned, recognizing that he was in the company of a cretin. "But, please—tell me how and why I ended up in hell, if that's in fact where I am."

"How about a hug first?"

"Pardon me?"

"I'm just the kind of person who feels that establishing physical contact allows me to open up more and to share intimacies."

"So how long have you been in therapy?" Edgy asked.

"All right, listen up," said the little man. "How'd you like the history of consciousness in a nutshell?"

Not as much as I'd like to see you in a nuthouse, Edgy thought. Nonetheless, against his better judgment, he said, "Fire away."

"There is evidence of direct linkage between the tiniest grain of sand and the needles on a pine tree. Between a squeeze bottle of pourable mustard in a Schenectady diner and a rock formation in a canyon in Utah. Between the position of the sun and David Duchovny's career choices.

"See, everything happens for a reason. We—"

Some unexpected physical contact—Edgy's fist meeting his jaw, a right hook that would have made Lennox Lewis proud—interrupted the man's train of thought.

"Yeah, thanks," Edgy said, walking away. "I read something about that once in a fortune cookie."

sundae with cherry

Here's a delicious, inexpensive way to satisfy your little one's sweet tooth. And big kids like it, too!

2 scoops ice cream
Hot fudge or chocolate syrup
Whipped cream
Maraschino cherry (optional)
Nuts (optional)

Scoop the ice cream into a bowl. Liberally drizzle with hot fudge or chocolate syrup. Top with whipped cream, and a cherry and nuts, if using.

SERVES 1 OR 2

what happens in hell
stays in hell

The next day, Edgy read the newspaper in the motel lobby. He found it odd that every article was written by Andy Rooney. Even more strange was the unmistakable smell of blood, sweat, and tears filling the air.

He looked up and saw, parked in front of the motel, a small bus of the type used to transport special-needs children to school. On the side was painted the words BLOOD, SWEAT & TEARS. Another mystery solved: the living members of the group had reunited—with the dead ones, quite possibly—for a two-week run at the Comfort Inn lounge. The opening act was John Denver.

Score one for hell.

But as he traversed a nearby field later that morning, Edgy not only smelled actual blood and sweat, he heard guttural grunting and the sound of boots marching on hard soil. For a minute, he thought he was reliving his wedding night with Marginelle.

The noises grew closer, and Edgy realized that he had stumbled into the center of a converging conflict.

"Nice shot, Captain Myron!" he heard, as the sound of pounding artillery drew nearer on each side. "Sergeant Irv—watch your back!"

Edgy had missed serving in several wars, after a botched operation as a youth had left him with a Franklin Mint collector's plate in his head (long story). But this was obviously an aggressive, full-on clash. In fact, it had the feel of more than a brawl— possibly a melee, or even a fracas.

Shots whizzed past his ears now. One hit a nearby tree and left a neon blue splotch.

Oh, great, Edgy thought. Paintball.

He could think of nothing more ludicrous than grown men spending thousands of dollars on ammunition and rifles that did nothing more than dirty the enemy's clothing.

Now the voices were within spitting distance. In fact, he could actually feel the moisture. "I reckon we're a-gonna take y'all in for a court-martial, Private Wendy," said a balding man in a Confederate uniform, his accent borrowed from a Des Moines dinner theater production of *Streetcar*.

"I need to reload," another adenoidal "soldier" whined. "Does anyone have any purple pellets?"

Okay, Edgy had to admit. Apparently there *is* something more ludicrous than paintball. And that would be a Civil War reenactment using paintball as weaponry.

"Hey, there," a shrill blond woman with a perfect manicure called out to Edgy. "Care to join in and fight for the Glorious Cause?"

"Appreciate the offer," Edgy said. "But I'd rather eat cat poo."

"I'll take that as a no," said the woman.

"Don't you people have children?" Edgy asked, as the two "armies" converged. "Or enjoy movies? Or needlepoint? Or drywalling? There are literally thousands of more interesting things to do on a Sunday."

"Well, that's your opinion," said a man sporting more epaulets than Michael Jackson let loose in the back room of a costume supply store with a hot glue gun. "But the American Civil War begs for reexamination. It was like a chess game with human beings. And every time we get together we learn more about this most unique and important conflict in American history, and maybe just a little more about ourselves."

"That Ken Burns thing wasn't enough for you?" Edgy asked.

"Come on, suit up," another Confederate paintballer urged, holding out a tattered and malodorous uniform. "We need another soldier to even out the teams. Phil Rabinowitz had a stomachache and had to leave."

"Maybe Phil was onto something," said Edgy.

What Patton should have said was "War *reenactment* is hell," Edgy thought, as he dusted himself off, left the battlefield, and headed toward town.

In the central square, a statue had been erected honoring the comedian Billy Crystal for "His Outstanding Contributions to the Arts." The sculpture depicted Crystal with eight arms; one waved to an imaginary audience, while the other seven patted himself on the back.

Edgy rinsed his face in a fountain and sat down. Then, realizing that he was sitting in the fountain, he found a bench.

He was ready for the truth. As unpleasant as this place was, it was crucial for him to know if it was The Great Beyond, in one form or another.

A man in his mid-twenties sat on a neighboring bench. He wore a T-shirt that read, IT'S ONLY FUNNY UNTIL SOMEONE GETS HURT—THEN IT'S *HILARIOUS*!!!

"Nice day," the guy said.

"Yeah, whatever," growled Edgy. "Listen, what do you know about this place?" he asked.

"Well, wherever you go, there you are," said the young man.

Edgy sniffed the air for marijuana and looked around for an open guitar case with some change in it but came up empty.

"I'm really not searching for philosophical guidance," he said, trying to stay calm, "so much as for hard facts."

"'Just the facts, ma'am,'" said the young man, doing a passable imitation of Sergeant Joe Friday from TV's *Dragnet*.

"You know, if I wasn't so tired, I'd take a swing at you," Edgy said, moving closer to the twenty-something. "You have to be the most annoying person who ever lived."

"Actually, I am," he said, extending his hand. "The name's Happy."

"Happy . . . ?"

"Camper."

"Happy Camper," Edgy moaned.

"Ten-four, good buddy."

"Wild guess: your 'thing' is to use idiomatic expressions that refuse to leave the lexicon—"

"That's the ticket!" Happy exclaimed. "But here's the good news. The half-full glass, if you will. You're looking at your tour guide through hell."

"You gotta be kidding. *You're* the guy who's making the official announcement that I'm in hell?"

"Guilty as charged."

"Could you freaking please–" Edgy started to ask, as politely as he could. "I'm trying to process this information . . . you think you could lay off the clichés for a few minutes?"

"Easier said than done," Happy replied.

So there it was. Now there was no question that Edgy was in hell. And apparently he had an escort.

"I guess you could say I'm the 'go-to guy' around here," Happy explained, lifting some corpspeak with the ease of a three-hundred-pound Russian doing the clean and jerk.

"Is there any way you could just even *slightly* curb the overused verbiage? You make the adjustment, and no one needs to know that we had this conversation, I promise."

"No sweat, amigo—I'm all about thinking outside the box," Happy said, wagging an index finger. "And no worries, mate—what happens in hell stays in hell."

You could hear Edgy's hand slap his forehead from a mile away.

"If I was a betting man," Happy said to Edgy as they strolled the midway, "I'd say you were feeling kind of confused right now."

"'If I *were* a betting man,'" Edgy corrected him. "If you use *if*, then it's *were*."

"*Capiche*—you're the boss," Happy replied. "But you get what I was saying, don't you, anyways?"

Edgy realized that he was being tested. As unpleasant as he had found his birth family, his wife, and virtually everyone he had ever come in contact with personally or professionally, Happy was in the running to top them all.

Still, maybe this bozo could help Edgy sort out his situation. Perhaps hell was a like a freeway, he thought, and leaving was just a matter of finding an exit.

"Let me help you sort out a few things," Happy began. "You're in hell, buddy. And if you're thinking that it's like some kind of freeway, and leaving is just a matter of finding an exit, well, you've got another guess coming."

wednesday's with happy

From the moment he saw the striped awning, Edgy knew that a meal at Thank the Lord It's Wednesday's, or T.T.L.I.Wednesday's, was inevitable. After a forty-five-minute wait, Edgy and Happy were shown to a booth.

"So," Edgy said. "I'm really looking forward to making some damn sense out of all this."

The waitress arrived. Judging from her complexion, Mike Wallace and Tommy Lee Jones had somehow conceived a child.

"And how are you gentlemen tonight?"

"Oh, livin' a dream," muttered Edgy.

"Can I start you off with a cold beverage?" she asked.

"Bring me a Moonlighting," Happy requested.

"Captain Morgan?" Edgy requested.

"Oh, we're a little slow tonight, so I think they gave him the night off," the waitress said.

"I meant the rum," Edgy said.

"Great, and then I'll tell you about our specials," the waitress said cheerfully.

"After you bring the bottle, you can take your time," Edgy grunted.

"I'm Clorette, by the way."

"And I'm nauseated," said Edgy as she skipped off.

"What's with you and upbeat people?" Happy asked.

"They're inauthentic," Edgy explained. "Look at this girl. She's slinging burgers at a chain restaurant. You'd think she'd just won the Powerball Lotto, yet she obviously doesn't have enough dough to buy herself a jar of Stridex.

"Plus, I'm here to have a conversation, not

watch her act out the whole frickin' menu. She wants to perform so badly? Go join Mummenschanz—don't waste *my* time."

"Jeez," Happy muttered. "Sorry I asked."

"Oh, God. She's back. Act Two."

"We have a wonderful steak tonight. It's been marinated in a mango vinaigrette, and—"

"Hey. Gwen Verdon. Skip the floor show, okay?" pleaded Edgy. "I just want a dinner salad."

"Great—let me tell you all about it! It's a crisp mix of iceberg and romaine lettuces, tomatoes, cucumber slices, and croutons. It's served with a homemade breadstick, and we'll add bacon for a small additional charge!"

Edgy sighed.

"What do you think of the fajitas?" Happy asked.

"Oh, I am, like, totally *addicted* to them," said Clorette. "They're chargrilled."

"'Chargrilled'? How is that different from 'grilled' or 'charbroiled'?" Happy inquired.

"Come freaking on," Edgy implored. "Who gives a rat's armpit?"

"Mum's the word—it's our own secret process," she said. "I *can* tell you that they're served on a bed of grilled onions and peppers, with black bean soup, Spanish rice, Colby cheese, guacamole, sour cream, pico de gallo, and warm flour tortillas. You can substitute steak for chicken, or we do offer a combo."

"Ay caramba! I want fajitas!" Happy said, closing the menu.

"Great—and save some room for our Cocoa Coma—that's two big slices of rich chocolate fudge torte layered with dark chocolate mousse, white chocolate mascarpone mousse, flourless chocolate cake, and Belgian chocolate ganache, topped with shaved white chocolate and served with a drizzle of raspberry sauce. I'd say it was heavenly, but we're not supposed to use that word—heh-heh. I hope my manager didn't hear."

"She obviously got the go-ahead to use every *other* word in the English language," Edgy said as Clorette left.

"Hey, the girl's lonely, she's worked a long shift, and she needs a skin peel pretty badly. Give her a break. Man, you got some issues."

"Agreed," Edgy said. "So, speaking of which—start talking."

"Chill out a little," Happy said. "My blood sugar is plummeting, I need to collect my thoughts, and—by the way—you ain't goin' anywhere, Pops."

"You are a source of great comfort," Edgy said.

Happy took a bite of bread and a deep breath before beginning.

"Think of it this way—death is the new life," he said.

"Is that supposed to make me feel better?" Edgy asked. "I'm not at all pleased with this turn of events. I mean, you've been dead for a while. I would imagine that I'll get used to it."

"It does grow on you," Happy acknowledged. "But you can never get complacent."

"That's absurd. You're dead. How much worse can it be?"

"Imagine tarring roofs for a living. You're on a slanted surface, high in the air, handling and inhaling hot poison all day."

"Touché," Edgy said.

"Imagine being the development executive

who decided that Keenen Ivory Wayans should have his own talk show."

"Okay, okay—I get it."

To change the subject, Edgy asked Happy about the circumstances of his demise. "I was hit in the head with a portable TV," Happy explained.

"By another human being? Or was it some freak accident?"

"I had a little disagreement with a salesman at Radio Shack, which ended with him hurling not just a Persian epithet my way, but a nine-inch Mitsubishi. You make the call."

What a way to go, Edgy thought. Getting skulled with a piece of low-end electronics. You can just never predict these things.

"You must have made him awfully mad," said Edgy.

"I suppose. And he had surprisingly good aim. How about you?"

Despite the fact that you're paying for dinner, I'd brain you with just about anything handy, Edgy thought. But that's not what Happy meant.

"How'd you go?"

"It was a cloudy day at a seaside amusement park. An extremely overweight woman boarded a malfunctioning roller coaster."

"Quite a setup," said Happy. "I'm thinking movie already. Or at least a Showtime Original."

"Are you serious?" Edgy asked.

"Well, I do have a little production company, and I've done a bit of screenwriting. Nothing that's actually been produced yet, but there's some interest . . ."

"You want the rights to my story before you've even heard it?"

"That's the way it's done—no guts, no glory," said Happy. He tilted his head at Edgy. "Hey—you ever acted? It would be a battle to get you network-approved for the lead, but has anyone ever told you that you look like that guy in *Midnight Cowboy*?"

"I hate to interrupt you, but I *was* going to tell you the rest of my story . . ."

"Bring it *on!*" Happy exclaimed, digging into his just-delivered fajitas.

"Well, like I was saying, it was a cloudy day at a seaside amusement park–"

"Yeah, yeah, so where's the money scene?" Happy urged.

"Jeez, you *are* like a studio executive," huffed Edgy. "Listen, here's the deal. Between you and me, there really isn't a lot of story. There is an 'inciting incident'–"

"Good, good–ya gotta hook 'em–"

"–which leads to windy discourses and dime-store theological speculation. We actually *see* the afterlife . . ."

Happy shifted in his seat. "You're losing me," he said. "When my ass starts to get numb, it's a sign. Either that, or this salsa's been unrefrigerated for too long."

"I wouldn't rule that out," said Edgy.

"All right, I'll try not to be such a buttinsky," said Happy, as he popped three capsules from a prescription container.

"Did you see *The Wizard of Oz*?" Edgy asked.

"Of course. Man, those flying monkeys–were they scary or what?"

"Yeah, yeah," Edgy said, humoring him. "Anyway, in this case, the fat lady was the house and I was the witch."

"You were the witch? *I* was Dorothy! My elementary school did a production of *The Wiz.* You'd be surprised how good I looked in braids and gingham dress."

"You do understand what I just said?" asked Edgy. "I mean, I was not only leveled by this moose of a woman, but I died in the process. Is it really appropriate to share your inconsequential memories of preadolescent amateur dramatics as I recount the details of my demise?"

"Sensitive, aren't you," Happy observed. "To the detriment of your auditory abilities, apparently. There's a reason I mentioned my outfit, nudnik. *Braids and a gingham dress?*"

Edgy choked on a crouton. "That—that's what I was wearing when I met Marginelle," he stammered. "Are you telling me that you're some kind of reborn version of my young self?"

"Maybe. Or maybe I'm a reincarnated Marginelle who's borrowing your clothes. Or just a guy who happened to wear the same outfit at some point in his life."

Happy leaned close to Edgy. "Pssst—does Dekaf Pawkchopp ring a bell?"

"Oh, I'm stuffed," said Edgy. "I was just about to go on South Beach when I died, but now, why bother? I've eaten enough carbs tonight to—"

"I was referring to the spiritual guru and healer, Dekaf Pawkchopp. He's someone whose teachings may not only help you figure out the afterlife, but the second and third acts of your movie, too."

"I'm not interested in adapting my life as commercial entertainment!" Edgy said as he stood.

"Oh, *sure* you're not. Like you wouldn't take some passive income."

"Passive income? I'm dead!"

"Exactly. That's what I'm talking about. A little F.U. money. The new Kias come out next month. I can just see you toolin' around in a Sportage."

"Truth be told," Edgy insisted, "I've always wanted to be a sportswriter. When I'm not tailgating and getting blotto at Raiders games, I'm actually a down-to-earth, spiritual seeker who appreciates simple pleasures."

"Oh, I love it." Happy smiled. "The network publicists are just gonna *eat you up*."

thursdays with larry

Moe is eleven years old. He is due for a haircut, and his mother takes him to a new barbershop. Looking at the magazines in the waiting area, he finds a style he likes in an article about the stylish coiffures of Pete Rose, film-maker Ken Burns, and Bill Gates.

The barber takes his scissors out of blue water that re-sembles engine coolant and sharpens the blades on a strop.

"Put this on his head," Moe's mother tells the barber, taking a spaghetti bowl out of her large handbag. "And then just cut around it."

"Coitainly!" says the barber, who Moe can see in the mirror has been bean-shaved. "Let me just call my assistant." In a bad French accent, he warbles, "Mistair Lar-eee . . .?"

Larry enters, and his hair is even worse. Moe is horrified to see that aside from wiry, Bozolike tumbleweeds sprouting from the sides, Larry is bald.

Taking the bowl from Moe's mother, Larry forcefully smashes it on the lad's cranium.

"Ooooh—oooh!" Moe shrieks. "My head!"

"Be a big boy, now, Moe," says his mother.

The chrome-domed barber—whose name, ironically, is Mister Curly—begins to cut. But rather than trim the hair, Curly pokes the sharpened scissors into Moe's neck. Blood spurts out onto Curly's and Larry's aprons.

"Hey—that smock was just washed!" Mister Larry complains.

"Go smock yourself! Woo-woo-woo-woo!" responds Mister Curly.

"Pick two," says Moe, extending his hands as the barber and his assistant lean down and examine them. Moe retracts all ten digits, save for the index and middle fingers. He then jams those four fingers into the barber's eyes, two fingers in each.

"Knuckleheads," says Moe proudly, as he knocks their skulls together, grabs his mother, and leaves.

about a blowhard

Edgy left Wednesday's full of not only their signature deep-fried Zucchini Zoomers, but internal conflicts that would undoubtedly inform the continuing course of his soul's journey.

If this was hell, how long would he be here? Was his life merely fodder for a television movie? If so, would the network air it for sweeps week? Could he get his name into the title somehow? Could it be released theatrically in foreign markets?

He knew that Dekaf Pawkchopp might have answers. The author of *You Don't Have to Sell*

Your Soul to Sell Out, Pawkchopp was a self-taught Buddhist-Presbyterian-Scientologist-Methodist-Catholic rabbi. Much of his renown in the spiritual community was due to Pawkchopp's having found not merely his "true self," but a tax shelter for his true self. All his books were best sellers, even the *True Self Cookbook,* which has been read on tape (unforgettably) by Steven Seagal. A notorious womanizer, Pawkchopp was rumored to have so many underage girlfriends that R. Kelly asked *him* for phone numbers.

Edgy journeyed to Ash Canyon, where Pawkchopp had built a luxurious complex featuring a meditation garden, a bodywork clinic, a bowling alley, and a world-famous grotto.

A tall, slender man in a caftan greeted Edgy at the gate.

"Can I help you?" the man asked.

"Let me in," Edgy implored. "Please."

"First time visiting Dekaf?"

Edgy nodded. The man handed him a clipboard.

"There's a fair amount of paperwork. The good news is that he'll work with your insurance."

"I pretty much got dropped from that policy when I died," Edgy said.

"Take your shoes off," instructed the man. "Then we need to check your chakras for lice. Following that will be a three-hour poetry chant, alternating verses by Ogden Nash and Jewel. Finally, you'll have a transfusion in which your blood will be replaced by decaf chai latte."

"As long as I don't have to drink it," Edgy said. "Stuff tastes like dirt."

Edgy sat in the meditation garden, which had obviously been converted from a go-cart track, and followed the caftan-man's instructions. When he was finished, the man approached again.

"Okay, here's the deal," he said. "I'm actually 'the guy.' The man you've come to see."

Edgy was amazed. Here was yet another random allusion to *The Wizard of Oz.* Even someone considered one of the deepest mystical thinkers of his time was reduced to tired pop-culture references and vaudevillian showmanship.

And yet, to be fair, there was respect to be paid. Pawkchopp was revered by virtually everyone Edgy had ever met. This was the man who in his lifetime had not only authored the bumper sticker "No Bozos," but had also—somehow—fathered five children with seven different women.

"So you're who I've come to see?"

"Yes," Pawkchopp said. "I'm a little shorthanded today. My assistants are out picking up some essential oils for me. And some conditioner. My scalp tends toward dry here."

"It is a great honor to meet you, Rabbi-Minister-Doctor Pawkchopp," Edgy said, bowing.

"Please. Call me Dekaf."

Pawkchopp led Edgy through the complex, passing along the way a geodesic dome that the holy man claimed was constructed entirely out of subscription

postcards he found in magazines he already sub-
scribed to.

They wound up in a basement lair Pawkchopp
called The Lowdown. There, they sat in expensive-
looking, uncomfortable chairs that were allegedly
good for the back.

"The concept of The Lowdown is simple,"
Pawkchopp explained. "Now that you have spent
some time in the underworld, we will measure
your tolerance of some basic elements found in
this particular region of the eternal afterlife."

"'This particular region'? Don't you mean
hell?"

Pawkchopp went rigid. "Let's try to avoid that
term. We're hoping Hot City will catch on."

"'Hot City'?"

"Yeah. I like it, but half the board is against it."

"Don't tell me—you're on the Chamber of
Commerce here?"

"This complex didn't build itself," Pawkchopp
explained. "Just getting the grotto zoned was a mon-
umental headache. Trust me—there wasn't enough

echinacea and goldenseal on the planet to get me through that *mishegas*. So. You all set?"

"I think so," Edgy said warily.

"Hands on buzzers."

"What?"

"Just kidding. Close your eyes. Can I put on some John Tesh music? Or Allan Sherman?"

"I wish you wouldn't."

"Fine. Keep your eyes shut."

Edgy complied, feeling an inner peace he hadn't experienced since learning that *America's Funniest Home Videos* had been renewed for a fifteenth season.

Pawkchopp began to speak, his voice a soothing if pungent balm.

"You are standing before a building which resembles a bank. But it is not a bank. It is actually a museum."

"A museum?"

"Right. As you enter, you see a football jersey, framed under glass. There's a hairpiece. A few marriage certificates. A nun's habit. One or two restraining orders."

"Okay," said Edgy, who was starting to think that this exercise was more confusing than a set of IKEA assembly instructions. "I'm visualizing, I'm visualizing."

"The jersey was worn in a motion picture called *Gator*. One of the marriage licenses is cosigned by Dinah Shore. Sally Field wore the habit in *The Flying Nun*.

"There's more. A pair of eighteen-wheeler mud-flaps used in *Smokey and the Bandit Two*. A video installation of Loni Anderson on *20/20* describing 'the love of her life.'"

"All right. I get the picture," said Edgy.

"Do you?"

"This museum is devoted to the life of Burt Reynolds."

"Correct." Pawkchopp squinted at his protégé. "How're you feeling right now?"

"Could I have a glass of water, please?" Edgy asked, as he tried to hide his disbelief. "So, let me get this straight. There—there's a Burt Reynolds museum?"

"Do lesbians drive Subarus?"

Edgy took a shaky sip of water and composed himself.

"And in case you think it's some kind of vanity deal," Pawkchopp continued, "Reynolds not only has one of Dan Marino's old jerseys displayed, but a signed copy of James Arness's autobiography."

"And the idea is that someone might venture there to see these things?"

"I haven't even mentioned the framed letter from Carol Burnett, or the key to the city of Buena Park, California."

Edgy felt a chill that Ted Williams would have envied.

"Let's move on. Did you hear about the group of slackers who were each tattooing a word on their bodies, hoping to create a full novel? Or were you aware that you can see televised bass fishing–somewhere in the world–at any hour? Did you know that there are restaurants charging twelve bucks for a *baked potato* because it's been rolled in rock salt? Or that there is actually a sequel to *Miss Congeniality*? Or that a woman with the last name

'Busch' is married to a man with the last name 'Wacker'? That a mumbling twentysomething American suspended himself over London in a Plexiglas cube for a month and a half and passed it off to the public as *magic*?"

"Get out."

"Finally, did you know this? In 1972, a crack commando unit was sent to prison by a military court for a crime they didn't commit. These men promptly escaped from a maximum-security stockade to the Los Angeles underground. Today, still wanted by the government, they survive as soldiers of fortune."

"Wait a minute," Edgy said. "That's the monologue from the opening credits of *The A-Team*."

"That's right . . ."

"Well, what does that have to do with anything?"

"I just wanted to see if you were paying attention," said Pawkchopp with a smile. "God, I love that show. George Peppard was never better."

The afternoon continued with a veritable pageant of curiosities. Pawkchopp produced a binder containing synopses of the projects Mel Gibson was planning to direct. He demonstrated the use of a multipurpose eating utensil called a "spork," which he claimed was actually patented in 1970. He produced a postcard featuring a photograph of the Liberty Bell recreated entirely out of wheat.

"Okay, I'm suitably creeped out," he told Pawkchopp. "But why are you telling me all this?"

Pawkchopp sipped his chamomile mocha and smiled kindly.

"That will be for someone else to explain," he said, bowing. "Wipe your feet on the way out."

ANOTHER SPECIAL MESSAGE FROM
AUTHOR RICH PABLUM

I'm not sure how you're feeling about the book so far, and I don't want to influence your reaction in any way, but I've got some freakin' goose bumps, here.

I mean, I knew this was a good idea for a story. But now I'm thinking big. I could get some keys to various cities for this. Honorary degrees from a university or two. An appearance on Nightline. *Or, better yet—that Jimmy Kimmel guy's show.*

As far as the food for the author tour goes, how would you feel about tapas? You know, little plates with, say, a broiled shrimp on it, or some roasted peppers with olive oil and pine nuts. It's light, and you can eat a little or eat a lot.

I wonder if Philip Roth and John Updike have to deal with this crap.

development hell

Edgy ventured back out, beyond the gates of Ash Canyon. The sky looked like the cover of one of those Dianetics books by L. Ron Hubbard. A pair of clouds resembling Tom Cruise and Kirstie Alley moved ominously toward each other. He heard a cash register *ring-ring* in the distance.

He thought about the exercise Pawkchopp had put him through. On the one hand it seemed as if he'd been in the company of a madman on whom herbal tea reacted no differently than a psychedelic drug. On the other, there seemed to be some sort of underlying message to Pawkchopp's theories that Edgy just couldn't comprehend.

The landscape before him was desolate, except for a large antenna dwarfing a shack with a sign reading AFTERLIFE BRAINWASHING CORPORATION. Edgy approached and knocked on the door.

"You have an appointment?" asked a voice from inside.

"I'm Edgy," was the reply.

The door opened and a thin but toned woman in a mannish business suit appeared. Edgy thought he recognized the scent of Brad Pitt's signature cologne, Ripe Pitt.

"Did you say you were edgy?" the woman asked. "Because we're looking for edgy for next season."

"I don't understand," he confessed. "I'm not even sure what business you're in. You're dressed weird and you smell funny."

"My name is Selma Soll. I am a clairvoyant, a transchannel, a psychic, and a medium. Although I can become a 'large' during the holidays—but who can't? Heh-heh."

Wow, Edgy thought. A psychic with a sense of humor. That's gotta be a first.

"I also greenlight programming."

"What do you mean, 'greenlight'? I've heard the term, but I'm not exactly sure what it means."

"I'm all about making quality television."

"'Quality television'? Sounds like an oxymoron—unless you work for HBO."

"I look for programming that will not only challenge people to look at and consider their own lives, but attract beer companies to pay six hundred grand per thirty seconds to show off bimbos in tight T-shirts."

"And does this pose any kind of moral dilemma for you?"

"Not really. They pay me really well, and I've got stock options."

"Well, I do have a story," said Edgy. "And there's been some interest in developing it . . ."

"Don't b.s. me," Selma said. "I need a name."

"Happy Camper?"

"Reasonably . . . I mean, I don't have a special man in my life right now, but—"

"No, that's his name. Happy Camper."

"Never heard of him. Does he own the rights to your story?"

"No, but he steered me toward a better understanding of it."

"Who's his lawyer?"

"I don't know," Edgy whined. "Can I please just tell you the story?"

"Start from the middle," Selma said.

She ordered a couple of pizzas, and Edgy recounted his experiences. She was surprised and impressed that he had actually made the pilgrimage to the complex of Dekaf Pawkchopp.

"He tell you about the Reynolds museum?"

"Yup," Edgy replied. "Blood-curdling."

"Let me ask you something," Selma said, with chilling solemnity.

"Okay," Edgy said warily.

"Are you gonna eat that last piece of mushroom?"

"Go ahead."

"All right, here's the skinny," she said. "Everything Pawkchopp described actually exists in the material world."

"What?" Edgy said.

"You heard me, mister. The Burt Reynolds and Friends Museum is in Jupiter, Florida. If you went to the northwest corner of Highway One and Indiantown Road, it's near the base of the bridge. You'd see a Chili's restaurant. Across from that is the Jupiter Eye Care Center. And right next to that is the museum."

"Wowzers. You're freakin' me out, here, lady."

"The spork? A staple at KFC. And I assure you, Mel Gibson *will* direct again. The twelve-dollar baked potato? Available at at least a dozen restaurants in Manhattan. The marriage of Busch and Wacker is the real McCoy, as are the tattooed-slacker novelists and the *Miss Congeniality* sequel. The bozo in the glass cube is named David Blaine. He mumbles when he's interviewed, he looks like he hasn't bathed in five years, and the only thing magical about him is that he can get a date."

"It's all real," said Edgy, letting it sink in. "Jeez.

That's crazier than a group therapy session with Lindsay Lohan and Courtney Love."

"And did Pawkchopp do the opening bit from *The A-Team*?"

"He sure did."

Selma smiled fondly. "I love that routine— never gets old. Listen, the point is this—you'd swear that everything Pawkchopp had you visualize would be exclusive to hell. But no. These are all events and phenomena involving people who are still alive, *allegedly* enjoying a better world than we are."

Selma's news caused a welcome relief to wash over Edgy. He felt a huge weight lift from his shoulders. It made him want to spend a day reading to the elderly, or rolling around on one of those inflatable silver exercise balls.

"So, you studied with Pawkchopp, too?" Edgy asked Selma.

"We went out for a while. But his obsessions wore me out. He's pretty taken with something he calls The Whole Schmear, a theory he developed after years of living on a commune with a group of Kazakstanian philosophers and acrobats."

"'The Whole Schmear'?" Edgy repeated.

"Basically, The Whole Schmear follows a belief that hell and heaven are much closer than people like Jerry Falwell and Pat Boone would have us believe."

"Sounds like sour grapes to me," said Edgy. "I mean, because he's here, and—"

"Take heaven—*please*," Selma said laughing. "No, seriously. Everything we know about heaven has been 'spun' by the powers-that-be in the Church, and by television shows like *Touched by an Angel, Charlie's Angels, Seventh Heaven*, et cetera."

"Have you ever even seen those shows, though?" Edgy asked.

"Has anyone? How about *Wings*—another one that spread false information."

"Okay, *Wings* was definitely not about heaven. In fact, it wasn't about *anything*, now that I think about it. As for *Charlie's Angels* . . . the TV show had nothing to do with heaven, and neither did the movies. The second one, if I remember correctly, was about Demi Moore showing off her awesome new boobs."

Selma ignored Edgy. "How about this whole idea of the weather in heaven? It's obviously foggy, twenty-four/seven."

"Hate to play devil's advocate—heh-heh—but those are clouds," Edgy countered.

"You see? You've been hoodwinked. Then there's the celestial music—*ugh*. Have you ever sat through a harp concert? Talk about a guaranteed sedative—I'd rather listen to Shaquille O'Neal read *War and Peace*.

"The only true thing about heaven that we have been fed by organized religion or the mainstream media comes from Victoria's Secret."

"Victoria's Secret? The lingerie store?"

"Exactly. Women do actually have large, firm breasts in heaven."

"Really?"

"Yup. They're issued Wonderbras upon arrival. Down here there's just an outlet store, you have to take a shuttle bus to get there, and the stuff has been seriously picked through."

Edgy was floored.

"That does explain a certain amount . . . like why Bob Dylan let them use his music for the Victoria's Secret TV commercials . . ."

"Now you're catching on. The Whole Schmear also incorporates a technique Pawkchopp developed for consciousness and personal transformation called Mindlessness," Selma continued.

"'Mindlessness'?" Edgy repeated.

"That's right, chief. Have you heard of this meditation practice where you pause for one minute, three times a day? The idea is that you just breathe, experience your being, and connect with the universe."

"Right . . ."

"Well, in Mindlessness, you don't do stuff like that. Mindlessness is about realizing that we are born alone and die alone, that Earth's resources are limited, that it's a dog-eat-dog, the-rich-get-richer kind of world. Otherwise, why would these expressions stand the test of time, while others are dropped from the vernacular faster than Paris Hilton's hip-huggers at a Tarantino wrap party?"

"Hold on," Edgy offered. "How about 'Do unto others as you would have them do unto you,' or all those, like, other, like, Commandment thingies?" Edgy's memories of his religious education were obviously fuzzy.

"'Do unto' . . . what was that again?" asked Selma.

"Forget it."

"Look, you're either gonna buy into this or you're not," Selma said. "Are we all connected? Maybe, but that's what lawyers are for. I mean, do you really *want* to be connected to that wheezing woman behind you on line at the airport? Or men with waxed handlebar mustaches? Or people who insist on explaining chaos theory to you at a cocktail party? Or the kid at the bowling alley whose job is to spray shoes with disinfectant? Or M. Night Shyamalan?"

"He did make *one* good movie," Edgy offered in the filmmaker's defense. "Look, I really think we're moving off the point, here."

"Which is?"

"I don't know. Are we all connected, or not? Are hell and Earth basically the same place? And where does heaven enter into all this? I thought *you* were the expert."

Selma paced her shack for a while. "I've got an idea. Let's interrupt the text one more time for some irrelevant filler, and then take a little walk. As we encounter people and sights you've been involved with over the course of your afterlife, it will all build to an emotionally satisfying climax for the audien—er, for you. For *you* is what I meant to say. Maybe we'll hear some dramatic but up-lifting music as well."

Edgy shifted his weight uncomfortably. "Why do I have this feeling that you're trying to create a montage?"

"Don't balk—montages are an effective way to manipulate the viewer."

"I just—I'm still not sure I see my story as a movie," Edgy said.

"*Television* movie," Selma corrected him. "What do you take me for, a whore?"

From: Rich Pablum
To: Atria Books

I guess you could say my "days" are numbered. Heh-heh.

When I realized that the book I pitched and sold to you was actually a rather unfocused, overly sentimental waste of wood fiber, I came up with a brilliant idea. I thought I could break up the narrative with short anecdotal memories of each day of the week.

Sadly, I am running out of days of the week.

With that in mind, I hope you will consider the following ideas:

LABOR DAY WITH JERRY
ONE-A-DAY WITH CALCIUM
START THE DAY WITH A SMILE
LIVE WITH REGIS AND KELLY
STILL LIFE WITH WOODPECKER
LUCY IN THE SKY WITH DIAMONDS

Help! I'm obviously struggling, here.

Rich

hell of an ending

"We've covered fallacies about heaven," Selma said as she and Edgy walked across a long footbridge over a canal teeming with industrial waste. "Now let's discuss Hot City."

"You know, if we're going to be at all honest with each other, we should call this place what it is—Hell."

"Fine," Selma said. "So tell me . . . what do people know of H—of Heh—"

"Say it—"

"—Hell."

Edgy pondered this as they entered the square with the Billy Crystal statue.

"That it's hot here. Unbearably hot."

"And have you found that to be the case?"

"I'm a little *schvitzy*, truth be told."

"But it's a dry heat," said Selma. "Honestly—my sinuses have never been better than since I moved here."

"What do you mean, 'moved here'?" Edgy asked as they entered the Brimstone Wal-Mart. "You don't *move* to hell—I was always under the impression that you're *sent* here."

"Another myth. The truth? Our Chamber of Commerce is doing a terrific job of promoting this place. 'Go to hell'? Ours. 'May you rot in hell' . . . 'Hell of a good book' . . . 'What the hell was I thinking?' . . ."

"You're telling me that these expressions were developed by copywriters to promote—what would you call it? Not 'tourism,' per se, but—"

"We call it Permanent Holiday."

"And yet, once you get here, you can't actually refer to the place as hell? Explain *that*."

"You're an artist, Edgy Kreep," Selma said with a forgiving smile and a gentle shake of the head. "You'll never get the intricacies of marketing."

Selma and Edgy sat at Java the Hutt and continued to talk.

"You two need anything?" asked the clerk as she wiped off a nearby table.

"No, thanks," said Selma.

"Super, then," the clerk said. Edgy noticed a slight resemblance to Marginelle that he hadn't caught before.

"Anything else you've heard about our fair borough?" Selma asked Edgy.

"What about the Devil?"

"The Devil is actually a guy named Stan Greenfield. And you know what he does? Big drum roll, here—he owns a grocery store."

"A grocery store?"

"Right. Deviled ham? Deviled eggs? Devil's food cake? It's a family business."

The case was mounting. Expensive baked potatoes and shrines devoted to fading movie actors were in the domain of the physical world. The underworld, conversely, had just been a victim of bad press and the ranting of religious zealots, borderline psychotics, information terrorists, and Republicans. The truth was that the climate was akin to that of Phoenix, and the so-called Devil was just a grocer named Stan.

Selma maneuvered her Kia Spectra through the park, then they pulled over, got out, and sat down on a bench.

A little girl toddled over. She could not have been more than three years old. She was unaccompanied by an adult. She had braids and wore a gingham dress.

The girl's piercing blue eyes riveted Edgy.

"What's wrong?" Selma asked.

"Look at this kid."

"Gorgeous. She could do commercials," Selma raved.

"That's not what I mean. It's as though she's looking through my soul."

"M.O.W.," the girl said.

Edgy got off of the bench and squatted down to the girl's level. "Omigod," he said.

"What?" asked Selma.

"She's telling me to make the deal on the M.O.W."

"Great! Let me call the network," said Selma, pulling out her cell phone and striding off.

"KIP-FAHR-IN."

"'Kip-fahr-in'?" Edgy repeated. "'Kip-far-in'? Oh, I get it. 'Keep foreign'—you want me to keep the foreign rights in the event that it plays theatrically overseas . . ."

The girl nodded. "KASHTING APPROOOOO-VAL."

Edgy pulled out a Palm Pilot he didn't even know he owned. He was catching on now. "I should get casting approval. Good point."

"RIIIIT . . . SKRIP."

"I should write it? Now, that's asking a little much. I mean, I've never written a script before . . ."

"TROW FIT!"

"Okay, I understand. If they say no, I'll throw a fit."

The girl smiled at Edgy, kissed him on the forehead, and toddled off just as Selma clicked her cell phone closed and approached.

"All right. We've got a deal," she reported. "They're going to bump *Hopeless Hausfraus* for a week and air the M.O.W. They've even got some interest from one of the kids on *The Baritones* for a supporting role. We have a start date in two months. All of that's the good news."

Edgy beamed. Then his smile faded as Selma took his hand and solemnly sat down beside him.

"What's the bad news?" he asked.

"We're shooting in Canada."

About the Author

Rich Pablum is the latest pseudonym for **BILLY FROLICK**. In previous incarnations he has authored *The Philistine Prophecy* (as McCoy Hatfield) and *Dumpisms* (as Horace Dump). A decade ago, as Ronald Richard Roberts, he spewed *The Ditches of Edison County* upon an unsuspecting public. Despite neither being adapted for the screen nor even read by Clint Eastwood, *Ditches* became a national bestseller.

Mr. Frolick's work has appeared in *The New Yorker*, *Premiere*, and the *Los Angeles Times*. He is coscreenwriter of *Madagascar*, a DreamWorks Animation film featuring the voice talents of Ben Stiller and Chris Rock.

If you can provide compelling evidence that God exists, define the word *postmodern*, or you just want to let him know what your favorite color is, Mr. Frolick can be contacted through the William Morris Agency.

Please note that all correspondence will become his exclusive property and may be used as the basis for a Lifetime movie starring Jamie Gertz.